For my publisher and friend Davy B.W..
For my son Davy B.S.

min𝑒dition
published by Penguin Young Readers Group

Text copyright © 2008 by Brigitte Sidjanski
Illustrations copyright © 2008 by Bernadette Watts
Original title: Der Fluss
English text adaption by Bernadette Watts
Coproduction with Michael Neugebauer Publishing Ltd., Hong Kong.
Rights arranged with "minedition" Rights and Licensing AG, Zurich, Switzerland.
Published simultaneously in Canada.
Manufactured in China by Wide World Ltd.
Typesetting in Poppl Laudatio by Friedrich Poppl
Color separation by Fotoreproduzioni Grafiche, Verona, Italy.

Library of Congress Cataloging-in-Publication Data available upon request.

ISBN 978-0-698-40077-1

10 9 8 7 6 5 4 3 2 1
First Impression

For more information please visit our website: www.minedition.com

Brigitte Sidjanski

The RIVER

Bernadette Watts

minedition

High in the mountains, where hardly any tree grows,
and where only mountain goats and snow hares can be seen,
a tiny trickle of clear water seeps out of the rock.

This streamlet ripples between big stones
and clumps of herbs until it comes to a place
where a lonesome pine tree grows.
The water bubbles merrily over its roots.
Five little pinecones peep down from their branches
and wonder where the dancing brook will go.
Then the cones pop off and —
plop! —
down they fall into the running water.
An adventure begins.

The little cones bob up and down excitedly.

Other brooks join in from other mountain peaks.

Together they form a stream that calmly flows

through beautiful countryside further down the valley.

What a wonderful world!

One of the pinecones thinks

this landscape is the best place in the world,

so he drifts over to the side

and washes ashore to his new home.

The four other cones continue their journey,
still wondering where the river will take them.
The water gets colder, and the cones feel snow falling.
Suddenly a sharp wind blows them across a frozen
mountain lake and tosses them around the ice.
The little cones enjoy it for a while,
but they begin to worry if the wind will ever stop blowing.
Could this be the end of their trip?

Finally the wind stops.

After many days of sunshine the ice melts.

The water is free to flow again,

carrying the pinecones to the other side of the lake.

Then — Look out, little cones! Too late! —

they fall right down into a deep gorge.

The river has become a roaring cascade.

The pinecones are so afraid!

What will happen to them?

One cone, however, likes the sound of all that roaring water,

so he bounces over into a small niche.

He wants to put down roots here in this dramatic place.

But the remaining three cones are glad when the river
leaves the gorge behind and begins to meander peacefully
through a kinder place.
The rough water is soon forgotten.
And this green valley is so peaceful that one little cone wants to
stay here. He has seen more of the world than he ever
dreamed he would, and now he feels that this is the
right place for him to stay.
Now there are only two cones on the river.

Further on, many more little streams join the river,
and it gets wider and stronger as it passes
through villages and farms.
The two remaining cones have a good time
bouncing on the waves and are happy to drift
toward whatever they find.
They look like little ping-pong balls
on the wide-open water.

The pinecones are in for more fun when a big river boat chugs by.

The boat makes waves, and the cones splash around.

One cone splashes up onto the riverbank.

He likes the feel of the cool mud here and decides to stay.

But the last cone decides to go on!

After many days the river enters a big city.

Now the water is deep and dark and full of strange smells.

The current is cold and strong. The last pinecone

is a bit frightened of this strange place.

He hears noises he has never heard before.

He almost wishes he had never set out on his huge adventure.

But he keeps floating on.

Suddenly he is lost in the darkness.

The little cone is relieved when the stream leaves the city behind
and takes him calmly through a very flat countryside.
The river passes between islands and rocks.
The water is very wide now.
It flows slower and slower and finally spills out into the sea.
The river has come to the end of a long journey.
It has been a long way from the tiny trickle of water
way up in the mountains.
Slowly the last pinecone drifts out into the endless ocean.

The little pinecone is the only one that traveled
all the way down the river, and he has enjoyed his great journey.
But he feels lost in this immense salty water.
For the first time he misses the sheltering mountains
back in his valley, on the pine tree.
Luckily a soft wave soon takes him to the shore.
Now he feels the warm sun on him, and he decides that,
finally, this is the place for him to settle.
But as he rests on the beach, the wind blows sand over him,
until he is completely buried.

No one can see the little pinecone anymore…

Or can they?